I0761165

THE CHORAL

also by Alan Bennett

plays

PLAYS ONE

(*Forty Years On*, *Getting On*, *Habeas Corpus*, *Enjoy*)

PLAYS TWO

(*Kafka's Dick*, *The Insurance Man*, *The Old Country*, *An Englishman Abroad*, *A Question of Attribution*)

THE LADY IN THE VAN OFFICE SUITE THE MADNESS OF GEORGE III
THE WIND IN THE WILLOWS THE HISTORY BOYS THE HABIT OF ART
PEOPLE HYMN and COCKTAIL STICKS ALLELUJAH!

television plays

ME, I'M AFRAID OF VIRGINIA WOOLF

(*A Day Out*, *Sunset Across the Bay*, *A Visit from Miss Prothero*, *Me, I'm Afraid of Virginia Woolf*, *Green Forms*, *The Old Crowd*, *Afternoon Off*)

ROLLING HOME

(*One Fine Day*, *All Day on the Sands*, *Our Winnie*, *Rolling Home*, *Marks*, *Say Something Happened*, *Intensive Care*)

TALKING HEADS TWO BESIDES

screenplays

A PRIVATE FUNCTION

(*The Old Crowd*, *A Private Function*, *Prick Up Your Ears*, *102 Boulevard Haussmann*, *The Madness of King George*)

THE HISTORY BOYS: THE FILM

autobiography

THE LADY IN THE VAN WRITING HOME UNTOLD STORIES
A LIFE LIKE OTHER PEOPLE'S HOUSE ARREST
KEEPING ON KEEPING ON

fiction

THREE STORIES

(*The Laying On of Hands*, *The Clothes They Stood Up In*, *Father! Father! Burning Bright*)

THE UNCOMMON READER SMUT: TWO UNSEEMLY STORIES
KILLING TIME

SIX POETS, HARDY TO LARKIN, AN ANTHOLOGY

THE CHORAL

Alan Bennett

faber

First published in 2025
by Faber and Faber Limited
The Bindery, 51 Hatton Garden, London EC1N 8HN
Typeset by Agnesi Text, Hadleigh, Suffolk
Printed and bound in the UK by CPI Group (Ltd), Croydon CR0 4YY

A CIP record for this book is available from the British Library

ISBN 978–0–571–39628–3

Printed and bound in the UK on FSC® certified paper in line with our continuing
commitment to ethical business practices, sustainability and the environment.
For further information see faber.co.uk/environmental-policy

Our authorised representative in the EU for product safety is
Easy Access System Europe, Mustamäe tee 50, 10621 Tallinn, Estonia
gpsr.requests@easproject.com

2 4 6 8 10 9 7 5 3 1

MAIN CAST AND CREW

Cast in order of appearance

ELLIS	Taylor Uttley
LOFTY	Oliver Briscombe
CHILD	Blake Bentham
MOTHER	Liz Simmons
WEEPING WOMAN	Fiona Organ
MARY LOCKWOOD	Amara Okereke
HERBERT TRICKETT	Alun Armstrong
JOE FYTTON	Mark Addy
ALDERMAN BERNARD DUXBURY	Roger Allam
MISS MUSCHAMP	Carolyn Pickles
MRS PEMBERTON	Angela Curran
BELLA HOLMES	Emily Fairn
GILBERT POLLARD	Thomas Howes
LAD AT AUDITIONS	Reuben Bainbridge
REVEREND CRABTREE	Ron Cook
MRS DUXBURY	Eunice Roberts
DR HENRY GUTHRIE	Ralph Fiennes
VIOLINIST	Alison Jones
VIOLIST	Josephine Wells
MISS NINER, CELLIST	Tamzin Griffin
ROBERT HORNER	Robert Emms
MRS BISHOP	Lyndsey Marshal
FLO	Roxanne Morgan
MITCH	Shaun Thomas
MATRON	Sally Rogers
CONVALESCENT OFFICERS	Ben Noble
	Benjamin Kirk
	Daniel Marles
PODGE	Christopher Dean
YOUNG WOMAN	Lauren Dickenson
SMALL KID	Ralph Falkingham
WOMAN WITH WHITE FEATHER	Ellie Sager
CURATE AT STATION	David Simon
CLYDE	Jacob Dudman

MAJOR DOBSON	Oliver Chris
CANON TRUELOVE	Malcolm Sinclair
LADY HORSFALL	Fenella Woolgar
MARY'S MOTHER	Cecilia Noble
DOCTOR	Mark Holgate
CHAUFFEUR	George Fenton
SIR EDWARD ELGAR	Simon Russell Beale
SINGING GIRL'S MOTHER	Aimée Maria Harris
SINGING GIRL	Anna Cook
SINGING VOICE OF MARY	Tia Jordan Radix-Callixte
SINGING VOICE OF CLYDE	Hugo Brady
SINGING VOICE OF DUXBURY	Donald Stephenson

THE CHORAL

SOPRANOS

Aimé Maria Harris Alexandra Cooper Alison Eastwood
Amara Okereke Emily Fairn Emily Pratt
Hrafnhildur Björnsdóttir-Parkes Jessica Hopkins
Joanne Dexter Lori Grainger Madeleine Wickham Brown
Mayuri Swaminathan Roxanne Morgan Ruth Pitman Jones
Suzi Saperia

ALTOS

Angela Curran Anne Henshaw Carolyn Pickles
Claire White-McKay Elizabeth Lincoln-Myers
Emily Harrison Josie Baker Julianne Coates
Lily Robson LucyAnne Fletcher Lyndsey Marshal
Matilda Hazell Merel Magali Cox Susan Beatty

TENORS

Christopher Dean Daniel Marles David Tomlinson
Jacob Dudman John Scholey Liam McNally Nico Shaw
Paul Dutton Peter Bates Richard Costain Roger Allam
Sammy Mills

BASSES

Alun Armstrong Angus Robertson Benjamin Kirk
Benjamin Noble Clive Spendlove David Hoult
Donald Stephenson Jonny Hill Mark Addy
Oliver Briscombe Phil Ramsden Ron Cook
Sam Meredith Shaun Thomas Taylor Uttley

'The Angel's' Farewell'
from *The Dream of Gerontius* by Edward Elgar
performed by Alice Coote and The Hallé,
conducted by Sir Mark Elder

Music Director and Coach to Ralph Fiennes
Natalie Murray Beale
Cast Music Director Tom Brady
Choral Music Director Joseph Judge

CONCERT SOLDIERS

Ashton Hall Benjamin King George Hann
Jonathan Aubrey-Bentley Luke Bedford Tom Afiyan-English
Tom O'Gorman Will Thompson

SALVATION ARMY BAND

Ashley Griffi Christian Lewis Jayne Griffin
Laurence Moorby Lydon Moorby

Directed by	Nicholas Hytner
Written by	Alan Bennett
Produced by	Kevin Loader Nicholas Hytner Damian Jones
Executive Producers	Eva Yates Caroline Cooper Charles Paul Grindey Charles Moore Phil Hunt Compton Ross
Director of Photography	Mike Eley, BSC
Production Designer	Peter Francis
Editor	Tariq Anwar
Costume Designer	Jenny Beavan
Make-up and Hair Designer	Erika Okvist
Music Directed and Arranged by	George Fenton
Co-Producer	Nicola Morrow
Casting Director	Robert Sterne
Additional Material by	Stephen Beresford

Developed in association with London Theatre Company

The Choral was presented by Sony Pictures Classics and BBC Film, in association with Screen Yorkshire, Head Gear Films and Metrol Technology

Preface

Alan Bennett

My plays and filmscripts have mostly come with an introduction. Gossip really, to do with the rehearsal of the play or the shooting of the film. With *The Choral* that wasn't feasible as I was incapacitated due to arthritis. My partner and I paid brief visits to the set in Harrogate and Saltaire, where we were made much of but were in fact no more than tourists. Or, worse, The Writer.

I felt on familiar ground because the film was set in Yorkshire and the West Riding. The forties were a golden era for the cinema, with Leeds, like most industrial towns, having dozens of picture houses sometimes changing their programmes three times a week. We went as a family, Dad, Mam, my brother and me, and with plenty of cinemas to choose from. The Lyric, The Palace, The Picturedrome and The Crown – and with generally a queue, invariably patrolled by an unsympathetic commissionaire bawling out 'two at one and nine', or 'three singles', the calls getting more urgent as it got nearer the time for the big picture.

These were remarkably varied both in subject and quality and, whatever the quality, not much fuss made. I would have seen umpteen Tarzan films (with Johnny Weissmuller) but I would also have seen without noticing it *Casablanca*, *Now, Voyager* and *The Red Shoes*. Just after the war, too, were a series of films set in the North. Admittedly, it was a North where the accents were noticeably wayward and would not get by today, post-*Coronation Street*, but there were some good actors: Tom Walls, Stephen Murray and (a bit of a strain) Dennis Price. I'm thinking of films like *The Master of Bankdam* and, set in Wales, *The Corn Is Green* and *How Green Was My Valley*. Labouring away during lockdown, I hoped that with luck *The Choral* might have a hint of these.

In my head I was writing a film I would have seen in the late forties. Though it was long before my time, the First War was still vivid in our family, as it must have been in umpteen others. My mother had lost her only brother Clarence at Ypres. He would have had his photograph taken like the soldiers awaiting their turn in Mr Fytton's shop, and it stood on the piano in my grandma's house off Tong Road in Leeds. Early in my career I had written about this photograph and had gone to Flanders to find his grave. Uncle Clarence was one of the few bits of family history we could claim. At the start of the war, he had wanted to join up but couldn't because he had a hernia, then a disqualifier, but women shouted at him in the street. Any operation at that time carried a risk but Clarence went into hospital and had the rupture mended (it only occurs to me now: where did he get the money to pay for the op?), so when he was killed in Flanders, Clarence was a volunteer. Dead long before I was born, he remains part of my childhood, dead but present at the Sunday musical evenings presided over by my Aunt Eveline, a fine pianist and once a performer in the silent cinemas, now reduced to housekeeping in Bradford. She would be joined at the keyboard by my father on violin and Uncle George on vocals, with a selection from Handel right through to Ivor Novello. As children, my brother and I couldn't wait for them all to end, whereas Grandma would have a little cry, Clarence's photo taken down out of respect.

Thanks to the Yorkshire Symphony Orchestra, by the time I was in my teens I was pretty well familiar with the classical repertoire. I couldn't play a note despite my father's attempts to teach me the violin, but on the night of Elgar's *Dream of Gerontius*, me and my sixth-former friends who normally sat behind the orchestra were displaced to make way for the chorus. We were disgruntled (and I remember being so) at having to sit in the dress circle. I was bored by the oratorio about an old man on the point of death and his struggle with eternity. But it must have sunk in because hearing it a second time when it turned up one weekend in Truro Cathedral during my National Service, I was swept away and have loved it ever since. So it was a natural choice when I started thinking of *The Choral*.

*

My thanks to Stephen Beresford, who was invaluable in smoothing out my sometimes awkward dialogue.

Introduction

Nicholas Hytner

The Choral is the fourth film Alan Bennett and I have made together. The other three – *The Madness of King George*, *The History Boys* and *The Lady in the Van* – started life on stage. *The Choral* was written for the screen.

It was pushed through my letterbox in a used jiffy bag on 25 March 2020 – the day before the first Covid lockdown – with a note attached:

> Scrappier than usual though at least it's typed, though by me so it's probably in parts incomprehensible . . .
>
> I've talked in general terms to George about it so even if you're not keen could you show it to him? I'm also not sure if manuscripts can be infectious . . .
>
> Bothering with a play at this juncture seems almost frivolous. I wish it were and then it might cheer things up.

It wasn't bulky (around fifty pages), unlike the first drafts of *The Madness of George III* and *The History Boys*, which were doorstoppers. But among the scraps, there were the bones of what made it onto the screen: a Yorkshire Choral Society in 1916 that has lost its chorus master and most of its men to the war, the recruitment of a new chorus master and a cohort of teenagers, the decision to rehearse *The Dream of Gerontius* and Elgar's attempt to cancel it.

Covid had thrown the future of the Bridge Theatre, which I opened in 2017, into doubt. For three years, I was focused mainly on its survival, borrowing money from the UK government's Culture Recovery Fund, spending too much by selling tickets to socially distanced audiences every time it was legal. Shows opened, then closed a few days later, either because we were all locked down again, or because someone in the cast tested positive and everyone else's phones went ping. I can't remember either the legislation or the technology behind the pinging, but it meant everyone had to go home. We'd have done better to stay dark – most theatres did – but at least it cheered things up.

It would have cheered things up even more if I'd thought *The Choral* was a play: a new Alan Bennett might have done wonders for our bottom line. But it was immediately clear to me that it should be a film, that there was a community at the heart of it rooted in a town that needed a concrete presence, that its structure was cinematic. Alan was easily persuaded that he was writing a screenplay, though he was never convinced anyone would make it.

It took four years to put it in front of the camera, which was partly my own fault – I had a theatre to take care of. Alan and I owe it to George Fenton (the George in his original note) that we persevered. George, who has written the score for all my films, has been Alan's friend for more than fifty years. He called me often to tell me there was something in it worth pursuing.

As draft followed draft, a line that never changed belonged to Guthrie, crushed by the news of his German lover's death at sea:

> Fucking war. The vicars want it. The women want it. The idiots getting killed, they want it. Who do you turn to?

I hope I have made a film that answers Guthrie's question. In the face of barbarism, you turn to art. The Choral's performance of *The Dream of Gerontius* doesn't shorten the war by a day, nor does it have any impact on what Ellis calls 'them in London' who make the decisions. But it's how the community who are its performers and audience explain to themselves what's happening to them. Music is more than solace: it asserts their common humanity even as their young men are slaughtered.

Clyde, mutilated and returned from the Front, wants no part of it because 'life's fucking shit'.

'So sing,' says Guthrie.

Originally, when Clyde reappeared, Bella went back to him. Among much else in the film, I owe to the playwright Stephen Beresford the observation that there'd be more to his story, and to Bella's, if he came back to find he'd been dumped. Why should he rejoin the Choral if it means seeing his ex-girlfriend?

The sight of Clyde in costume is what tips Elgar over the edge, and in the first draft when he cancelled the performance, it stayed cancelled. This might have worked on stage, though most theatres would already have called time on the participation of a chorus of fifty. Alan wasn't keen when I insisted that the show had to go on. Perhaps it could happen behind closed doors, to bypass Elgar's veto? An audience of 'friends and family' was where we found common ground.

By this time, I'd realised how at home I felt with *The Choral*. I spent much of my Manchester childhood and adolescence singing in choirs: the North of England in 1916 doesn't feel alien to me. I have worked with professional musicians throughout my career, in theatres and opera houses. The Ramsden Choral Society unites mill owner with mill workers: undeniably utopian, but my experience of music is that it knows no boundaries. (Though it must be said that since 2010 the UK Department of Education has done its best to put them up by removing music, drama and art from the curriculum.)

The film deals only obliquely with the miserable working conditions Duxbury's mill workers must have endured: it is more interested in how they flourish when they discover the elation of communal music-making. And it implies, I hope, that the more challenging the music is, the greater the satisfaction in conquering it.

Alan came to the classical repertoire in the 1940s and '50s through The Yorkshire Symphony Orchestra. I discovered it in the '60s and '70s, every Sunday night at the Manchester Free Trade Hall where the Hallé Orchestra played under John Barbirolli. As my school occasionally provided a boys' choir for the Hallé, I was once conducted by Barbirolli. I still own a CD of Mahler's Third Symphony on which I'm part of the children's chorus that mimics the joyful sound of church bells (*Bimm Bamm Bimm Bamm*) in the movement entitled *What the angels tell me*. Mahler's angels promise eternal bliss to all mankind, untouched by the agony foretold by the Angel who ushers Gerontius into Purgatory.

The Hallé under Barbirolli were supreme in Elgar (as they were in Mahler), and they remain so now. Barbirolli's recording of *The Dream of Gerontius* was for decades the one to have; it is rivalled by the same orchestra's more recent version under Mark Elder, which we use at the end of *The Choral*, finally allowing the audience to hear why Elgar might have been enraged by the Ramsden re-orchestration.

I didn't sing much Elgar when I was a chorister, though I was part of a madrigal group that used to sing *As Torrents in Summer*, a beautiful *a cappella* chorus from a piece discouragingly called *Scenes from the Saga of King Olaf*. It has lyrics by Henry Wadsworth Longfellow; their sanctimonious piety wouldn't be out of place on a Victorian sampler. Cardinal Newman, who wrote the long poem Elgar set to music in *Gerontius*, is Milton in comparison.

Handel had a surer touch with his librettists, and I included his music as often as I could. My career on the London stage began with a production of his opera *Xerxes* for English National Opera. *Where'er You Walk*, which Clyde sings to Guthrie for his audition, is sung in the opera *Semele* by a philandering Jupiter to his high-maintenance mortal lover – the words are by Congreve. (By 1916 it had become a de-sexed parlour ballad. Either way, it comes with me to my desert island.) When Handel writes religious music – like *Angels Ever Bright and Fair*, Mary's audition piece – I want to believe. But I prefer the Choral's 'less religious' approach to *Gerontius* to Elgar's own.

An irony of Elgar's afterlife is his association with an image of England that was embalmed in *Land of Hope and Glory*. You can find him on YouTube, conducting it at the opening of the Abbey Road Studios in 1931, but he was dubious about it, as he is in the film. He was contemptuous of many of his British musical contemporaries, and was, like Guthrie, a passionate Germanophile: he was overjoyed when Richard Strauss called him 'Meister'. He was as dismayed by the First World War as he was by the rise of the Nazis, repelled by Hitler's persecution of the Jews. Many of his best friends really were Jewish: a relief not to have to make the usual excuses for a great English artist's casual bigotry ('needs to be taken in the context of the prejudices of his time').

The Elgar of *The Choral* isn't the whole story. His father was a piano tuner and shopkeeper, and he was Roman Catholic – the British establishment was slow to accept him. He wrote his greatest music in the first decade of the century and was understandably resentful when he fell out of critical favour. But he was certainly vain and touchy, and as he grew older, his pursuit of young women became more conspicuous.

He wouldn't have been the first artist to have tried to stop a performance of his work that fell short of what he expected, though in my experience it is the posthumous keepers of the flame who are the worst control freaks: try deviating even a little from Samuel Beckett's stage directions. Elgar wrote *The Dream of Gerontius* for an orchestra of around a hundred and a double chorus of anything up to two hundred. You can see why he might have baulked at a heavily cut version for piano, Palm Court trio and Salvation Army band.

Still, my sympathies are with the Choral. I have spent a career in the theatre reworking the classics for whatever circumstances prevail. Copyright notwithstanding, great art becomes public property. Guthrie is right to adapt *Gerontius*, Mary is right to demand that the show goes on, and Robert is right to put it in costume – though the idea of staging it as a series of tableaux from the Western Front occurred to me only a few weeks before we shot it. Infinitely more mischief is made with the repertoire every night of the year in the world's opera houses.

The Salvation Army band's involvement was another late addition, after George Fenton despaired of doing anything like justice to Elgar with only four players, though his musical arrangements throughout the film are so inventive I'm sure he would have managed. He, like the editor Tariq Anwar, goes back with me to *The Madness of King George* in 1994. It was the first time I've worked with the director of photography Mike Eley, the production designer Peter Francis and the costume designer Jenny Beavan. I could direct *The Choral* only by being in their orbit.

The very young actors were all new to me (Robert Sterne was the casting director who found them), but among the rest were actors I've known for decades, many of them at the National Theatre when I was its Director. I've done Shakespeare with at least five of them: Roger Allam, Mark Addy, Lyndsey Marshal, Simon Russell Beale and Ralph Fiennes. Ralph's whole-hearted involvement in *The Choral* was why my fellow producer Kevin

Loader and my agent Anthony Jones were able to put together the money to make it. Michael Barker, of Sony Pictures Classics, never wavered in his enthusiasm for it since I told him about it over breakfast in Manhattan in the autumn of 2023.

Alan writes in his Preface about the photograph on his grandma's piano of his Uncle Clarence, killed at Ypres. The pictures I remember from my childhood were of my very much alive grandfather and his brother, in Second World War army and RAF uniforms.

But I have a photo from just after the First World War of my father's uncle, Barnet Goldberg, in the uniform of Captain Corcoran, commanding officer of Gilbert and Sullivan's *HMS Pinafore*. Barnet Goldberg was a stalwart of the Manchester Jewish Amateur Operatic Society. He was born in the early 1880s outside Warsaw, so the Captain of the *Pinafore* must have sung with a Yiddish accent. I imagine the Manchester Jewish Amateur Operatic Society would have drawn the line at *The Dream of Gerontius*: Cardinal Newman's fevered visions of Purgatory are now disowned even by the Vatican. But the amateur musical culture that thrived a century ago on both sides of the Pennines survives, and the singers who make up the Ramsden Choral Society come from all over Yorkshire and Lancashire. *The Choral* is their film: they are its eponymous heroes.

The Choral

EXT. MUDDY LANDSCAPE – DAY

Subtitle: 1916

A desolate landscape. Rain. Sporadic gunshots. What one briefly takes to be the Front turns out to be a shooting party on the moors. Lofty and Ellis are beaters, Lofty tall, skinny and innocent, Ellis more sophisticated. Both eighteen or so.

ELLIS

I can't see the trenches can be any worse than this. It's diabolical.

EXT. ROAD – DAY

We see them cycling home through the rain, below them Ramsden – a Yorkshire town with rows of terraced houses, mills and factories. Swinging from Ellis's handlebars, a pheasant.

LOFTY

Nice of them to give us a bird.

ELLIS

When they've shot two hundred, yes, very generous.

EXT. POST OFFICE, RAMSDEN TOWN CENTRE – DAY

Later. Ramsden High Street. A Salvation Army band is playing. Ellis reading a notice in Post Office window. Lofty appears, now a telegram boy.

ELLIS

Which way are you heading?

LOFTY

I'm on official business.

ELLIS

I'll hang back when you're door knocking.

Ellis is still scrutinising the notice.

They're taking on down at the Choral. Open auditions.

They start to walk away.

LOFTY

Blame the war. No men.

ELLIS

Blame it? Class barriers coming down. About time.

Ellis runs with his bike and mounts it, pedalling fast, laughing. Lofty chases after him, laughing too.

EXT. RAMSDEN TOWN CENTRE – DAY

Lofty and Ellis cycle towards the next delivery; behind them looms Duxbury's Mill.

ELLIS

Fat chance of a revolution here.

LOFTY

Ramsden?

ELLIS

England. We're fodder for the mill and we'll be fodder for the Front.

EXT. ROW OF WORKING CLASS HOUSES – DAY

Lofty and Ellis stop outside one of the houses. Lofty gestures at Ellis to back away. Ellis eyerolls and wheels his bike further back. Lofty knocks.

CHILD
(*calling*)

Mam!

His Mother appears. Lofty gives her a telegram. She pales.

LOFTY

Sorry, missus.

CHILD

Who's it from, Mam?

MOTHER

(*quietly*)

The King.

She pulls him inside as Lofty and Ellis cycle off.

EXT. ANOTHER STREET – DAY

Lofty knocks. The door opens. A woman takes the telegram. She starts weeping and kisses him before going inside.

Ellis joins Lofty.

ELLIS

Could've got in there.

LOFTY

No. Do you think?

ELLIS

Grief. It's an opportunity.

Ellis rides on, Lofty stares at the house for a moment before following.

EXT. RAMSDEN TOWN CENTRE – DAY

Lofty and Ellis cycle past a Salvation Army band, playing on a street corner, six of them including Mary wielding a tambourine.

Across the street is the Undertaker's. Herbert Trickett, sombrely dressed, emerges with a score of the St Matthew Passion *and crosses to Fytton's Photographic Studio. Lofty and Ellis swerve to avoid him.*

TRICKETT

Watch where you're going! Hooligans.

INT. FYTTON'S PHOTOGRAPHIC STUDIO – DAY

Two or three soldiers in uniform having their pictures taken by Joe Fytton. Trickett waits.

TRICKETT

How many's that?

FYTTON

Twelve, fourteen. I've lost count. Mind you, it's a special rate for recruits.

TRICKETT

I'd be coining it if they fetched them home.

FYTTON

Who?

TRICKETT

The dead. I'd be laughing.

FYTTON

Nay, Herbert.

TRICKETT

(*holding up the score*)

Auditions. Be sharp.

Fytton finds his score and they hurry out.

EXT. RAMSDEN TOWN CENTRE - DAY

Fytton and Trickett walk past Ellis and Lofty, who are getting back on their bikes, Lofty now without his uniform. Salvation Army band still playing.

TRICKETT

(*to Lofty*)

Young man.

LOFTY

Mr Trickett?

TRICKETT

Aren't you in the choir at St Wilfred's?

LOFTY

I was.

TRICKETT

What happened?

LOFTY

My voice broke.

TRICKETT

Can you still sing?

LOFTY

A bit. Why?

FYTTON

Mr Trickett and me are both in the Choral.

TRICKETT

On the committee.

FYTTON

We're having auditions. Now.

TRICKETT

At the Jubilee Hall.

LOFTY

Him and me?

TRICKETT

Anybody.

(*to Ellis*)

Can you sing?

ELLIS

I can dance too if called upon.

TRICKETT

Not in the *Matthew Passion.*

FYTTON

(*going*)

Don't be shy. We won't eat you.

TRICKETT

I might.

EXT. REHEARSAL ROOM – DAY

Outside the Jubilee Hall, Lofty and Ellis wheeling their bikes.

ELLIS

Not keen, quite honestly, and anyway they reckon to be quite choosy. Although now there's no night school I'm going to be at a loose end.

LOFTY

What happened to night school?

ELLIS

No teacher. Joined up. Still I don't fancy this. Singing. Not me.

LOFTY

Me neither.

Mary (*in her Salvation Army uniform and bonnet*) *appears.*

MARY

Excuse me. Is this where they're doing the auditions?

ELLIS

I believe it is, yes. In fact we were just going in ourselves, weren't we?

The three of them go in.

INT. REHEARSAL ROOM – DAY

A handful of auditionees at the side, waiting their turn – more women than men. At the far end of the room, Flo, a young woman is doing her audition. Members of the committee – including Trickett, Fytton and a clergyman – Reverend Crabtree – sit listening.

Mary comes in, followed by Ellis and Lofty. Alderman Duxbury, the Chairman of the Choral Society, turns and sees her.

DUXBURY
(*hissing under the music*)
Not today, thank you. We're busy.

MARY
I've come for the audition. Mary Lockwood.

FYTTON
(*the kindest of the committee*)
Of course, take a seat, young lady.

DUXBURY
(*mutters to Fytton*)
I thought she was collecting. They always are.

Mary moves to the side, pressing herself against the wall. Ellis and Lofty come and stand beside her.

ELLIS
It's your bonnet, it puts them off.

She ignores him. Pointedly.

Do you never take it off?

MARY
No.

ELLIS
Not even in bed?

Mary goes to sit with some women, including Miss Muschamp and Mrs Pemberton.

MISS MUSCHAMP
We're contraltos. Are you a contralto?

MARY
I'm . . . I just like to sing.

MISS MUSCHAMP

Well, you belong over there. We're not auditioning, are we, Vera?

MRS PEMBERTON

No, we're longstanding. We're the backbone. And singing is social, no nonsense about democracy. I don't want to be singing next to my window cleaner.

Mary walks away and sits next to Bella, who smiles at her.

Pollard, the Chorus Master, is at the piano (a baby grand).

FYTTON

Thank you, Miss Proctor. Miss Holmes, you're next.

Bella gives Pollard her sheet music. Ellis elbows Lofty in the ribs.

ELLIS

(*sotto voce to Lofty*)

Oh, hello . . .

FYTTON

(*whispers to Pollard*)

This is Clyde's girlfriend. Missing in action.

Fytton looks at her with a sympathetic smile.

POLLARD

(*to Bella*)

Any news?

Bella shakes her head.

FYTTON

He was the best tenor we ever had.

BELLA

Was? He's only missing. It's not been confirmed.

FYTTON

(*hurriedly*)

Oh yes . . . he'll turn up.

Ellis turns to Lofty, smiling and shaking his head.

ELLIS

(*sotto voce to Lofty*)

Not yet, I hope.

Lofty is amused but also appalled.

Bella sings (with a powerful voice) the beginning of the chorus of a music-hall song, 'A Little of What You Fancy Does You Good'. Duxbury stops her.

DUXBURY

(*shocked*)

There are one or two new faces in the hall today, and that's . . .

FYTTON

(*whispering up at Duxbury*)

You should introduce yourself.

DUXBURY

What?

FYTTON

(*whispered*)

Tell them who you are.

DUXBURY

They know who I am.

FYTTON

No. Here.

Duxbury takes this in.

DUXBURY

I'm Alderman Duxbury and you all know me from the mill. Only this isn't the mill. It's the Choral and we're all equal here.

ELLIS

(*sotto voce to Lofty*)

Oh yeah.

DUXBURY

The person you've got to watch out for isn't me. It's the Chorus Master, Mr Pollard. Keep on the right side of him and you won't go far wrong.

Pollard smiles politely.

The point is . . . Should you be lucky enough to be selected, you will be expected to comport yourselves accordingly. I hope I make myself plain?

BELLA

Oh, don't worry, Mr Duxbury, I've got a sacred side.

Duxbury turns on one of the lads waiting to audition.

DUXBURY

I mean you, lad, you're black bright.

LAD

I've come from the mill.

DUXBURY

Whose mill?

LAD

Yours.

INT. REHEARSAL ROOM – DAY

Later. The Committee – Duxbury, Fytton, Trickett, Reverend Crabtree, Pollard – are the only ones left in the room.

DUXBURY

Joining up? Why now?

POLLARD

I feel it's my patriotic duty.

DUXBURY

They keep reckoning to bring in conscription. Why not wait for that? It'd still be patriotic.

Silence. No one expected this response – least of all Pollard.

What about these today? Do we take them or not?

POLLARD

The Salvation Army lass is good.

DUXBURY

It's not lasses we want.

POLLARD

The lads are all right.

DUXBURY

All right? All right? This is the Choral.

POLLARD

(*now ready to go*)

Good strong voices. They just want a little encouragement.

Standing now, Pollard pauses, looking as though he could use a little encouragement himself.

Well, this is it . . . I suppose I'd better . . .

He goes around the other men, shaking hands.

DUXBURY

I hope he puts more wind up the Germans than he ever did the sopranos.

EXT. REHEARSAL ROOM – DAY

Pollard is walking down the street.

DUXBURY

Gilbert.

Pollard stops and turns, pleased to see him. He rushes back to shake Duxbury's outstretched hand.

And think on, Gilbert. Don't be the first.

POLLARD

At what?

DUXBURY

Fighting. Anything.

Pollard nods, smiles.

POLLARD

Don't worry about me, Mr Duxbury. Too smart to get shot.

Almost as soon as he's said that his face looks stricken.

Oh God, that's not to say . . . I don't mean—

DUXBURY

Nay, lad. Off you go. Good luck.

Pollard nods and goes, quickly. Duxbury watches him disappear.

INT. FYTTON'S PHOTOGRAPHIC STUDIO AND SHOP – DAY

Pollard in uniform. The flashbulb goes off and he stands, frozen.

INT. DUXBURY'S HOUSE – NIGHT

The parlour of a substantial house on the edge of town. Tea things, a grand piano. The committee is suggesting names for a possible chorus master, a replacement for Pollard.

REVEREND CRABTREE

Arthur Fox?

Trickett tips his elbow, indicating he drinks.

Neville Widdop?

DUXBURY

No grip. The Choral needs grip.

TRICKETT

There's always Irvine Price.

DUXBURY

Not for me there isn't. Divorced.

FYTTON

I'm going to say a name.

They all look at him.

But I don't want to be shot down—

DUXBURY

Who's shooting you down?

FYTTON

No one. Yet. But when I open my mouth—

The parlour door opens – Mrs Duxbury is standing in mourning black. Duxbury speaks in the firm, flat voice usually employed with children.

DUXBURY

What's the matter, Margaret?

MRS DUXBURY

I heard voices.

Reverend Crabtree smiles at her, benignly. Fytton sits back down. Trickett busies himself with the paperwork.

DUXBURY

(*patiently*)

It's the Committee, love. I told you. We're looking for a new chorus master.

FYTTON

Pollard's gone and joined up, the great barmpot.

A moment while everyone absorbs this blunder. Mrs Duxbury doesn't react. She seems numb.

DUXBURY

Go upstairs, love. We'll not disturb you.

She leaves. Silence. Duxbury exhales.

Go on then, Joe.

FYTTON

What?

DUXBURY

Your name. Spit it out.

FYTTON

Dr Guthrie.

A beat while this is processed.

DUXBURY

What?

FYTTON

Henry Guthrie.

DUXBURY

No. No. No.

FYTTON

He's back.

DUXBURY

I dare say he is.

FYTTON

And, frankly, in other circumstances he wouldn't even consider the likes of us.

REVEREND CRABTREE

Isn't Guthrie—?

FYTTON

Yes.

DUXBURY

He's been living and working in Germany. By choice.

FYTTON

He had musical opportunities. You could understand it.

DUXBURY

He had musical opportunities here. But he preferred Germany as having better choirs.

TRICKETT

Treachery.

FYTTON

He worked wonders at Leeds.

TRICKETT

He was despised. Folk were terrified.

REVEREND CRABTREE

He's an atheist. That's why Leeds got rid of him.

FYTTON

Well, there are atheists now. There's one in Bradford.

DUXBURY

Not conducting the *Matthew Passion.*

He sits at the piano.

FYTTON

I heard his Mozart *Requiem.*

DUXBURY

So did I. It was wonderful.

He plays a chord. Lets it hang in the air.

FYTTON

You never said.

TRICKETT

We can't, Joe. Not if his sympathies are German.

REVEREND CRABTREE

Besides, there was talk of other things.

FYTTON

What other things?

REVEREND CRABTREE

Let's just say I'd prefer a family man.

FYTTON

You'd prefer the Archbishop of Canterbury.

Duxbury turns from the piano stool. Mind made up.

DUXBURY

He'd never come anyway. He'll be conducting somewhere they don't care about his peculiarities. Liverpool.

FYTTON

He's not. He's playing at the Queens' Hotel.

INT. QUEENS' HOTEL - EVENING

It's closing time. The quartet – piano and string trio – playing their final piece. Henry Guthrie, the pianist, is playing with great aplomb. A couple of ladies in the café are lingering to hear the very last drop of his genius.

At the door, Fytton and Duxbury, watching.

Guthrie finishes and acknowledges the ladies' applause with a stately nod.

INT. COLLINSON'S CAFÉ – EVENING

Fytton and Duxbury talking to Guthrie as chairs are placed on top of tables. Fytton has already succumbed to fandom. Duxbury takes a different approach.

FYTTON

You're wasted here.

A waitress is clearing a table and Guthrie nicks a plate of eclairs.

GUTHRIE

I like it here. It has perks.

As the violinist and cellist depart –

Good night, ladies.

FYTTON

We've lost our chorus master.

Duxbury flashes him a look – giving it all away so early.

GUTHRIE

(*shakes his head*)

Those days are over.

DUXBURY

Why?

GUTHRIE

I have a living to earn.

DUXBURY

We all have livings to earn. This is England.

The truth of the problem has been inadvertently revealed.

Guthrie smiles a little.

(*lowering his voice*)

Look, this isn't . . . You have to realise – If we were to offer you the post—

GUTHRIE

(*amused*)

If!

DUXBURY

We'd be taking a real risk. You lived in Germany.

FYTTON

For several years.

GUTHRIE

And that disqualifies me from conducting a choir?

DUXBURY

I'm trying to be reasonable—

GUTHRIE

Oh, is that what you're doing?

DUXBURY

I'm offering you an opportunity. The *Matthew Passion* at Ramsden Town Hall. Only . . . We have to have peace of mind. What did you do it for? And where do you stand?

GUTHRIE

With regards to the *St Matthew Passion*?

DUXBURY

With regards to the war.

Guthrie considers for a moment.

GUTHRIE

'A man should hear a little music, read a little poetry, and see a fine picture every day of his life, in order that worldly cares may not obliterate the sense of the beautiful which God has implanted in the human soul.'

FYTTON

Oh, that is nice. Who said it?

GUTHRIE

Johann Wolfgang von Goethe.

DUXBURY

For God's sake, man. Lower your voice.

GUTHRIE

Why did I stay there? Wouldn't you stay in a country of civilised, cultured people? People who put music and beauty – art – at the centre of everything they do? The English think music is just social life carried on by other means. I don't. I think it's important.

Duxbury stares at him. We can see that he absolutely would. But he can't say that.

FYTTON

See? It was musically motivated.

GUTHRIE

I would need to have control.

DUXBURY

Control?

GUTHRIE

Creatively.

DUXBURY

Well, I'm the Chair – that can't change. And I always . . .

(*corrects himself*)

I find I'm most often called upon to sing the tenor solos.

GUTHRIE

Well . . . no point disrupting the choir any more than is necessary.

Duxbury nods, gratified. They understand each other.

I should want to bring my own pianist.

DUXBURY

Unpaid, mind. We'd be doing him a favour. We're doing you both a favour – let's face it.

FYTTON

Not half as big as the favour you're doing us.

INT. REHEARSAL ROOM – DAY

A crowd of singers, more women than men. One or two of them watching out for Guthrie through the window.

MRS PEMBERTON

Where do they say he's from?

MARY

He's not from anywhere. Only he went and lived in Germany.

MISS MUSCHAMP

I'm afraid this is the end. I shall be obliged to leave.

ELLIS

He travelled – so what? People do.

LOFTY

We don't.

MRS PEMBERTON

He was interviewed.

LOFTY

By who?

MRS PEMBERTON

A policeman.

MISS MUSCHAMP

They took him to Ripon.

ELLIS

Aye, and found nothing amiss – So here he is.

MISS MUSCHAMP

If they found nothing amiss then explain his behaviour in the public library.

ELLIS

What behaviour?

MISS MUSCHAMP

He goes in and reads the papers. All of them. Every morning. And when he's done – and Miss Pendle goes to smooth the sheets . . . they're always opened at the same page.

A shout of 'He's coming' and they disperse. All except those held by Miss Muschamp's narrative . . .

LOFTY

What page?

MISS MUSCHAMP

The Naval Report.

INT. REHEARSAL ROOM – DAY

Guthrie strides in, followed by his young assistant Robert; also the Committee – Duxbury, Fytton, Trickett and Reverend Crabtree. The chorus are back in their seats.

GUTHRIE

Is this everybody?

FYTTON

Pretty much.

GUTHRIE

(*incredulous*)

For the *Matthew Passion*?

He walks down through the seats: there are around twenty-five women and twelve men. He shakes his head in despair. He addresses the chorus.

'Mein Vater, ist's möglich, so gehe dieser Kelch von mir.'

There is an audible gasp. Some people murmur, outraged.

'My father, if it is possible, allow this cup to pass from me.' Although, no doubt you sing it in English.

DUXBURY

We most certainly do.

Guthrie sighs and turns to Robert. Duxbury is waving down little murmurs of dissent.

GUTHRIE

This is Mr Horner. He will be playing for today's auditions.

A further ripple of consternation.

LOFTY

I thought we'd done the audition.

GUTHRIE

Not for me you haven't. And that goes for everybody.

DUXBURY

(*outraged*)

We're on the Committee.

GUTHRIE

No exceptions.

FYTTON

I haven't anything prepared.

GUTHRIE

Scales will do.

FYTTON

Scales! Us?

TRICKETT
(*under his breath*)

He was your choice.

Mrs Bishop enters. She is a striking woman – plainly disliked by the more strait-laced members of the choir.

MRS BISHOP

Not too late, am I?

A little gasp of horror from some of the ladies . . .

INT. REHEARSAL ROOM – DAY

Mrs Bishop is auditioning – something religious. She has a good voice.

MISS MUSCHAMP

She's shouldn't be singing this. It's sacrilege.

MRS PEMBERTON

Disgusting.

INT. REHEARSAL ROOM – DAY

Miss Muschamp is now auditioning. Also something religious ('To Be a Pilgrim') – but not half as good.

Guthrie nods, dismissively, as she comes to a finish, glad it's over.

Trickett's next.

Later: Mary sings. Guthrie looks over to Robert, delighted.

INT. REHEARSAL ROOM – DAY

Duxbury is addressing the chorus. Guthrie, seated, Robert at piano.

DUXBURY

Well, that was . . . a stimulating afternoon . . . I'm sure I speak on behalf of the entire society when I—

He looks at the entire society, and unsure of a round of applause he changes tack.

The fact is – the Town Hall is booked and the word is out. The *St Matthew Passion* will be performed in just a few short weeks . . .

CHORUS MEMBER

Aren't Bacup doing the *Matthew Passion*?

DUXBURY

They were, only their Jesus went and joined up. It's a bit of an old warhorse but it's a piece we know. Some of us can do it with our eyes closed.

GUTHRIE

I would like to hear the chorale 'O Haupt Voll Blut und Wunden' – 'O Sacred Heart Sore Wounded'. Eyes open, if you please.

A flurry of page turning. Guthrie moves round the chorus listening to the individual singers.

A brick comes smashing through the window.

Don't stop. Don't stop. Sing on.

They come to the end of the verse. Everyone rounds on the brick. Trickett picks it up, wrapped around it a note.

Any message?

TRICKETT

(*reading*)

It says, 'Hun muck.'

DUXBURY

Bach? 'Hun muck'? Bach? Call the police.

GUTHRIE

I wouldn't bother. The way you were singing, it was probably a critic.

INT. REHEARSAL ROOM – DAY

The Committee is gathered round the piano. Other chorus members queueing for tea.

DUXBURY

He is German, I suppose.

ROBERT

(*Guthrie's piano player*)

Who?

DUXBURY

Bach.

GUTHRIE

So, that's it, is it? Even sung in English, Bach is out.

TRICKETT

Bricks through the window. There's a danger to life and limb.

DUXBURY

Never heed. There's plenty of alternatives.

GUTHRIE

Such as?

DUXBURY

Beethoven, obviously.

GUTHRIE

German, obviously.

REVEREND CRABTREE

Handel.

ROBERT

He ended up English, but he started off German.

GUTHRIE

I suppose it depends how much of a pedant our brick thrower is.

FYTTON

Mendelssohn.

GUTHRIE

German.

TRICKETT
(*devoiced*)

And Jewish.

GUTHRIE

There's Brahms, of course, whom I have met, but he alas is also a Hun.

He marches off. Duxbury follows.

INT. REHEARSAL ROOM – DAY

At the tea urn . . .

ELLIS

We could be in the pub now instead of hanging about here arguing the toss.

LOFTY

He's a bit posh is that pianist.

MARY

He's refined.

FLO
(*territorial*)

That's what I said. I said he was refined.

Ellis approaches Bella, standing alone.

ELLIS

Any news?

Bella doesn't say anything.

BELLA

My mother thinks you know. She thinks . . . if you love someone . . . you can just tell.

ELLIS

Do you?

She looks at him.

BELLA

Which?

ELLIS

Know.

She shakes her head. Walks away. Ellis watches her go.

INT. REHEARSAL ROOM – DAY

Guthrie stares out of the window.

DUXBURY

Did you really meet him?

GUTHRIE

Who?

DUXBURY

Brahms.

Guthrie looks at him now.

GUTHRIE

I had that privilege.

(*turns back to the window*)

Although it was in Germany, so you may not consider it a suitable topic for conversation.

DUXBURY

What was he like?

Duxbury is genuinely interested, moved even.

GUTHRIE

'Frei aber einsam.'

DUXBURY

Eh?

GUTHRIE

'Free but lonely.' It's . . . something he wrote. I wish

we were doing his *Requiem*. Then they'd really have something to throw bricks about.

DUXBURY

There must be someone people don't object to.

GUTHRIE

Have you considered, Mr Duxbury, that it might be me that folk object to – just as much as the music.

DUXBURY

That's as maybe. But you're our chorus master.

Guthrie is warmed slightly by this.

Only . . .

GUTHRIE

What?

DUXBURY

For God's sake, man, rein in the bloody German.

Guthrie is struck by an idea –

GUTHRIE

Elgar.

DUXBURY

Eh?

GUTHRIE

Elgar.

He walks back toward the piano. Duxbury follows.

INT. REHEARSAL ROOM – DAY

At the piano.

TRICKETT

Him from *Pomp and Circumstance*?

GUTHRIE

Amongst other things. He started off as an organist, same as me.

DUXBURY

Have you met him as well?

Guthrie shakes his head.

GUTHRIE

This is Elgar.

Guthrie plays a few bars of The Dream of Gerontius.

FYTTON

That's right enough.

GUTHRIE

'Right enough'? In Germany he's a god: he's up there with Wagner.

FYTTON

Elgar?

GUTHRIE

It isn't all marches. He did an oratorio a few years back. Premiered in Birmingham Town Hall. *The Dream of Gerontius*.

TRICKETT

News to me.

GUTHRIE

The audience hated it. If it hadn't been religious it would have been booed off the stage. I liked it.

ROBERT

Why did they hate it?

GUTHRIE

Hadn't been rehearsed properly. Of course, Gerontius is a tenor.

He plays another section for Duxbury's benefit, singing the tenor line himself. (*He sings poorly, like most conductors.*)

DUXBURY

Could we do it?

GUTHRIE

In terms of permission? Or skill?

DUXBURY

Either. Both.

GUTHRIE

I shall write to him. And meanwhile, we have to face facts. It needs a huge chorus and male voices are at a premium. We must recruit.

He strides toward the lads. Duxbury following.

DUXBURY

Fine. Only no riff-raff.

GUTHRIE

Do you want a choir, Mr Duxbury, or do you want a Sunday School?

He has gone over to the group of younger choir members at the tea table.

Have you got any pals who can sing?

ELLIS

Does it matter where? I've got one sings in a pub.

GUTHRIE

He can sing in a brothel so far as I'm concerned.

Miss Muschamp overhears this. Turns to Mrs Pemberton.

MISS MUSCHAMP

Well, that really is the final straw.

As Guthrie approaches he beams at the ladies.

GUTHRIE

Excellent work today, contraltos.

Miss Muschamp beams back. Ice cracked.

MISS MUSCHAMP

Thank you, Dr Guthrie.

GUTHRIE

Now, surely some of you ladies know a gentleman or two who might be suitable to swell our numbers?

MRS PEMBERTON

There's my husband.

GUTHRIE

Does he sing?

MRS PEMBERTON

He'll do as he's told.

EXT. PUB - NIGHT

Guthrie, Ellis and Mary are on their way to the pub after rehearsal. (Also Lofty, Bella and others.)

ELLIS

You're not coming in?

MARY

I certainly am. I'm used to pubs. I just wave my tin.

INT. PUB – NIGHT

Five men at the bar are bawling out 'It's a Long Way to Tipperary'. Guthrie walks past, listening. He points to one of them – Mitch.

GUTHRIE

He'll do. And these three too.

When Mitch stops, Ellis introduces him.

ELLIS

Mitch, this is Dr Guthrie.

MITCH

Doctor? Why? Who's poorly?

ELLIS

From the Choral.

MITCH

Oh. Well they won't want me. I live down Theaker Lane.

GUTHRIE

I don't know where people live. A choral society shouldn't mirror the social order. It should transcend it.

MITCH

(*to Mary*)

Are you in it?

MARY

I might be.

MITCH

I like the way you rattle your tin. Makes me want to put a penny in your slot.

MARY

Yes and me to give you a crack across your face.

She walks away.

ELLIS

She doesn't like you, Mitch.

MITCH

Well, I'll have to join the choir then, won't I?

The men at the bar start another song, Mitch joining in. It continues under the next scene.

EXT. THE HALL – DAY

Guthrie and Robert approaching The Hall, a small stately home that has been converted into a military hospital.

ROBERT

Haven't you done it before? *The Dream of Gerontius*. Why did you not say?

GUTHRIE

Because it was in Nuremberg.

This seems to deflate Robert a little.

ROBERT

Seems like everything good that happened to you, happened in Nuremberg.

Guthrie isn't rising to that. Robert is embarrassed for having said it.

Will he give his permission?

GUTHRIE

Who?

ROBERT

Elgar.

GUTHRIE

He will if I write to him. The man may be our greatest living composer but he's a fellow musician, however grand. Artists are like that, Robert. They notice each other. They connect.

Guthrie marches up the steps. Robert waits behind.

ROBERT
(*to himself*)

Not all of them.

Guthrie rings the bell.

INT. THE HALL – DAY

The Matron of the hospital walking Guthrie and Robert towards the ward.

MATRON

Sing? They're not in a state to sing, most of them. What have they got to sing about? They're convalescent. They don't want to waste their energy on singing.

They've reached the door. She pushes it open.

INT. THE HALL, WARD – DAY

Guthrie and Robert stare at the men on the ward. It's a sobering, pathetic sight – disfigured, injured, broken young men. The matron claps her hands as she addresses the ward.

MATRON

This gentleman wants to know if any of you can sing.

Two or three hands go up hesitantly; one of the men is blind.

GUTHRIE

Have you got a piano?

INT. THE HALL, DRAWING ROOM – DAY

In the drawing room, the three volunteers round a posh grand piano crowded with family photographs. Robert is playing.

Three injured soldiers – one a man in a wheelchair – are singing 'Three Little Maids from School' fairly raggedly, but enough to please Guthrie.

EXT. A BAKERY – DAY

As 'Three Little Maids' continues, Guthrie and Robert walk down the High Street and turn into a Bakery.

INT. A BAKERY – DAY

Podge is baking bread and is covered in flour.

ELLIS

Podge. This gentleman wants to know if you can sing.

PODGE

Sing what?

GUTHRIE

Anything. Surprise me.

Podge goes on baking while he's singing – handing round newly baked buns, too.

(*stopping him*)

Not bad.

PODGE

The song?

GUTHRIE

The bun. We can work on the other.

INT. REHEARSAL ROOM – DAY.

Rehearsal in progress: there are as many men as women, the total number now around fifty. Choir singing 'Praise to the Holiest'. Sopranos slightly flat. Guthrie stops them.

GUTHRIE

Sopranos flat. 'Praise to the Holiest.'

They sing it again.

Still flat! 'Praise to the Holiest.'

Ellis turns to Lofty.

ELLIS

(*under*)

Again?

Guthrie has superhuman hearing, it seems.

GUTHRIE

Again.

EXT. DUXBURY'S HOUSE – DAY

The sound of Duxbury singing.

INT. DUXBURY'S HOUSE PARLOUR – DAY

Duxbury sits at the piano, working his way through the score. He's singing and following very slowly with one finger on the keys . . .

INT. PUBLIC LIBRARY – DAY

Guthrie is standing before the daily papers spread out under the green lamps.

He hesitates before he turns over a page revealing a report on the Naval battle of Jutland:

'SEA BATTLE RAGES ON – HUGE LOSS OF LIFE'.

He quickly closes it.

GUTHRIE
(*whispered*)
Stop . . . stop . . . stop . . .

At the counter, he is observed by Miss Pendle, the Librarian.

EXT. TOWN HALL – DAY

A large poster is being hung on the board outside the Town Hall: MILITARY SERVICE ACT 1916. EVERY UNMARRIED MAN OF MILITARY AGE, *etc.*

Lofty (*in telegraph-boy uniform with another sheaf of telegrams*) *and Ellis are reading it, both with bikes.*

LOFTY
(*hopefully*)
Mam says there'll be deferment.

ELLIS
What for? Singing in the choir? They're all old, that's why. Them in London. They decide it. Old and well off. When we go makes no difference to them.

LOFTY
That's not very patriotic.

ELLIS
I'm patriotic but in my own good time. Carted off to France. I haven't lived.

LOFTY

That's what ought to get you deferred.

ELLIS

Living?

They ride off.

EXT. SULLIVAN STREET – DAY

Lofty calls at an ordinary house, Ellis waiting on the bike. Mrs Bishop comes down the street.

ELLIS

Don't look now but there's Mrs Bishop.

LOFTY

Why won't the other women sit with her at the choral?

ELLIS

Why do you think?

(*very polite*)

Hello!

MRS BISHOP

Do I know you?

ELLIS

You might be more familiar with the sound of me, Mrs Bishop, rumbling underneath you.

MRS BISHOP

(*tersely*)

I beg your pardon?

ELLIS

The Choral. I'm a bass. My mate here's a tenor.

She walks away.

(*calling after*)

Perhaps we'll meet in a less formal setting soon.

MRS BISHOP

Don't count on it. Cheeky sod.

EXT. MILL DAM – DAY

Lofty and Ellis have met Mitch. They're walking towards the mill dam, all wheeling their bikes.

LOFTY

It's not fair.

MITCH

What?

LOFTY

Having to go at eighteen. Not having done it. I can't be the only one. No fuck, no Front. That ought to be the decider.

MITCH

Well, I've done it and it doesn't make it any more acceptable, though I think once you're over there they cater for all that.

LOFTY

Do they?

MITCH

Brothels apparently.

ELLIS

Well, that's something.

LOFTY

But it oughtn't to be just intercourse, not having slept with someone. There's other stuff.

ELLIS

That's right. I've never tasted champagne.

MITCH

I have. It's muck.

LOFTY

I've not been in a proper motor car. I've never even seen the sea.

ELLIS

You've been to Morecambe.

LOFTY

It wasn't in that day. I don't want to throw it away on anybody. I'd like to . . . bestow it.

ELLIS

You could always bestow it on Mrs Bishop. Only she charges, even for bestowing.

They jump in. Two or three other boys are already in the water.

EXT. MILL DAM – DAY

On the other side, Bella, Mary, Flo and two or three others are watching, their feet dangling in the water.

BELLA

Can you swim?

FLO

Don't know. Never felt the need.
(*to Mary*)
Mary'd have to take her bonnet off.

BELLA

Don't you start. She gets enough of that from Mitch. Do you like him?

MARY

(*watching Mitch*)
A bit. He can swim. Look at him.

BELLA

Clyde and me used to come down here on a night with nobody about. Not even a cossy. He was that bonny.

MARY

(*looking at Mitch*)

I don't want to know.

BELLA

You do. I can tell. Anyway he's dead. You don't want this, being left. The others never leave you alone. Ellis is right enough but it's only because I'm available.

FLO

Cheer up. We've got the Queens' Hotel to look forward to. Guthrie's treating all the new recruits to their teas.

MARY

The recruits? What about us?

FLO

Not recruits to the army, stupid. Recruits to the choir. All of us.

EXT. CANAL TOWPATH – DAY

All the young choristers ride their bikes back to town, singing together as they go. Their singing continues under the next scene.

EXT. QUEENS' HOTEL – DAY

Guthrie walks down the street. Unbeknownst to him, there's a gang of small kids following him. After a moment they pick up small stones and dirt from the road and pelt him.

He turns in shock to see them running away. One stops for a final fling of muck.

SMALL KID

(*shouts*)

Fuck off, Fritz!

And he's gone. Guthrie dusts himself down.

INT. QUEENS' HOTEL – DAY

Fytton and Duxbury coming into the Queens', every table occupied.

FYTTON

This is grand. You'd never think there was a war on.

Except there are several wounded soldiers among the clientele.

As they make their way to their table, Trickett, in his undertaker gear, leads in a funeral party.

Is it a funeral?

TRICKETT

Well, it's not a wedding.

FYTTON

Is the tea thrown in?

TRICKETT

With a civilian funeral, of course it is. And it's the first I've had in a fortnight. It's tragic. Everybody's bereaved and I'm going bankrupt – it breaks your heart.

Later:

Crowded round a table: the new choir members, Duxbury and Fytton. Guthrie has taken his place with the string trio.

DUXBURY

You see, this is what we're fighting for.

FYTTON

Egg custards?

ELLIS

(*to Mitch*)

Don't get overexcited, only your friend's divested herself of her helmet.

And Mary has indeed taken off her bonnet and is dancing with Bella.

MITCH

What's she dancing with Bella for? There's plenty of men. She could be dancing with me.

ELLIS

Do you dance?

MITCH

That's beside the point.

On the dance floor . . .

BELLA

Does Mitch not dance?

MARY

No. Thank goodness.

BELLA

I'd like to dance with Ellis, only folk would make remarks.

Bella looks over, sees Ellis blowing her a kiss.

Mary . . . Am I terrible . . . ?

MARY

Why?

BELLA

I almost wish the telegram would come. Then everyone would know that Clyde was dead and I'd be . . .

She shrugs.

Back at the table:

DUXBURY

Eat up, lads.

They are wiring into their teas when a woman comes up and hands something to Ellis.

ELLIS

What's this?

WOMAN

Why aren't you at the Front? Why aren't you fighting?

ELLIS

Because I'm singing. We all are. And when we're called up we'll go. So in the meantime, madam, you can take your flaming feather and use it to tickle your fanny, because nobody else is going to.

The woman bursts into tears.

LOFTY

You shouldn't have said that.

MITCH

Well, she shouldn't be accosting folks.

LOFTY

Only she lost her brother. I took the telegram.

INT. QUEENS' HOTEL – DAY

The room is emptying, chairs are being put on tables. Guthrie has joined the choir.

FYTTON

Will you tell us a bit more about the piece? Some of us are still a bit in the dark.

He goes to the piano, where the string trio are packing their instruments.

GUTHRIE

It's a simple story. As the name suggests, Gerontius – Mr Duxbury – is an old man who in the first part of the oratorio is on his deathbed. It's quite short and ends with his death. In the second part there is some delay while the destiny of Gerontius' soul is decided.

ELLIS

You see, you always have to queue. Heaven'll be the same.

Bella laughs. Ellis catches her eye.

GUTHRIE

In this case it's because the forces of good and evil are contending for Gerontius' soul, with the music given to the demons very dramatic, while the angel . . . that's Mary—

MITCH

In her bonnet.

GUTHRIE

Which she could be – after all, the Salvation of Gerontius is what she wants.

Mary beams at this.

ELLIS

(*sotto voce to Mitch*)

And you wanting the other.

GUTHRIE

To cut it short, the Angel wins and the oratorio ends with her conveying his soul to purgatory, with a promise to lead him from there into the presence of God.

ELLIS

Not much of a story, is it.

FYTTON

You don't have to believe it. I always took the *Matthew Passion* with a pinch of salt.

GUTHRIE

The words, of course, are very beautiful. John Henry Newman.

Guthrie starts to read from the score - but he knows it pretty much by heart.

'Farewell, but not for ever brother dear,
Be brave and patient on thy bed of sorrow;
Swiftly shall pass thy night of trial here,
And I will come and wake thee on the morrow . . .'

DUXBURY

Wait a minute? Newman? Cardinal Newman? A Catholic?

FYTTON

What difference does it make? He could be a Mohammedan. We haven't even asked him.

DUXBURY

Who?

FYTTON

Elgar.

GUTHRIE

Yes, we have.

Everyone looks at Guthrie. A ripple of surprise.

DUXBURY

And what did he say?

GUTHRIE

He hasn't replied.

DUXBURY

Catholics, you see. Feckless.

He plays a few passages. Everyone silent and still, lost in their own worlds.

At the back, we see Ellis taking Bella's hand in his. She doesn't resist. She looks up at him and smiles.

EXT. REHEARSAL ROOM – DAY

The sound of the choir rehearsing through the open windows.

INT. REHEARSAL ROOM – DAY

The choir singing, Duxbury (as Gerontius) solo on top of them – Sanctus Fortis. *Guthrie stops him.*

GUTHRIE

Mr Duxbury. You are not singing. You are crooning. And contraltos – have you anything against B flat? No? Well, you never go anywhere near it.

Mitch is staring at Mary. Ellis nudges him.

ELLIS

Wake up. If she's ever daft enough to go out with you, she'd still have God as her fancy man.

MITCH

All right for you. You've latched yourself on very nicely.

Ellis gives Bella a wink. She pretends to be annoyed, smiling.

Worst of it is. I only just found out her second name. Elspeth.

ELLIS

So?

MITCH

You're never going to get anywhere with an Elspeth. Elspeth? It's impregnable.

Lofty arrives in his pillbox. Everyone hushes at the sight.

GUTHRIE

You're late.

Lofty seems especially buoyant. Is he carrying a newspaper?

LOFTY

Never mind that, Dr Guthrie. They've sunk the *Pommern*!

A ripple of confusion and questions from the choir; most don't know what that means.

It's a German battleship! Eight hundred and thirty-nine Fritzes dead and floating in the North bloody Sea!

A huge cheer. But not, we notice, Guthrie . . .

He is stunned. He stares straight ahead. Everyone else embracing. The only person to notice Guthrie is Robert – who seems to understand but can't leave the piano.

He's being whacked on the back by choir members urging him to play. He starts up the National Anthem, still staring at Guthrie.

Lofty comes up to Guthrie with a telegram. Shouting over the noise –

(*shouted*)

Sorry. I forgot. This is for you, sir.

Guthrie takes it, numbly. Lofty is enveloped into the joyful throng. Guthrie tears it open and looks down:

'GERONTIUS. DELIGHTED. ELGAR.'

Guthrie stares down at it, while the choir sings and cheers and embraces.

INT. REHEARSAL ROOM – DAY

Later. The choir singing. It's patchy, to say the least. Guthrie holds up his hand.

GUTHRIE
(*coldly*)
If only you sang Elgar with the confidence with which you sang the National Anthem.

Robert plays the notes.

The choir struggles through it. They stop, and Robert plays on. Duxbury realises he was expected to continue –

DUXBURY
Have I to go on?

GUTHRIE
I think that was Elgar's intention, Mr Duxbury.

Robert goes back. Duxbury – nervous, anyway – makes a pig's ear of the section: Sanctus Fortis. *Guthrie hammers his hands down on the lectern. Silence. The choir look at each other. The uncomfortable silence continues.*

INT. REHEARSAL ROOM – DAY

Mary and Robert working on the score at the piano. Duxbury sitting alone, miserable.

MARY
Are you all right, Mr Duxbury?

DUXBURY
You get discouraged. I just wish I had a better voice. I enjoy it so much.

MARY

No . . . it's a nice voice.

DUXBURY

I'm sure everybody thinks I'm only singing Gerontius because I put my hand in my pocket.

MARY

No.

DUXBURY

It's true. Art depends on money. Without the mill there would be no choir. No mill, no music.

MARY

I'm sure people are grateful.

DUXBURY

I don't think they are. Not when I'm always putting my spoke in. But I pay for the flaming choir. That entitles me to some say. I just wish – you mustn't say I said this – I just wish he wasn't so . . .

MARY

It's just his way. And you can sing.

Duxbury goes.

ROBERT

He can't. Not very well.

Mary looks at him, sadly trudging away with his tea.

MARY

He lost his son.

EXT. REHEARSAL ROOM – EVENING

Mary, Flo and Robert leaving the hall.

MARY

Do you know anything about Elgar?

ROBERT

Not much.

MARY

He's coming to Manchester the day of the concert. It was in the *Argus*. They're giving him an honorary degree. I thought . . .

ROBERT

What?

MARY

If we wrote to him he might come over for the performance. I was going to ask Dr Guthrie.

ROBERT

I wouldn't.

MARY

Why?

ROBERT

I just wouldn't, that's all. He won't be grateful. He never is.

He walks on, leaving Mary a little bewildered. Flo follows after him.

FLO

What's the matter, Robert?

ROBERT

I got my papers this morning. The call-up.

FLO

Oh, Robert . . .

They stand like that for a second before he starts to walk again.

I wish you liked girls like the other lads do.

ROBERT

What's that supposed to mean?

FLO

Mind you, if you did . . . Lasses probably wouldn't like you so much. Sad, isn't it?

She watches him go.

EXT. TOWN-CENTRE STREET – NIGHT

Robert wandering the streets, disconsolately. He sees Guthrie sitting on a bench, looking grief-stricken. He watches for a moment, then walks towards him . . .

EXT. PARK BENCH – NIGHT

Robert and Guthrie on a park bench.

ROBERT

Perhaps he wasn't on board.

Silence. Guthrie shakes his head.

GUTHRIE

Joined up in the first wave. Practically first in the queue. At least you've got more sense.

Robert looks down for a second.

ROBERT

Was he . . . Did he play music?

GUTHRIE

He had a good voice. Unspoiled. Hansel. As Gerontius he would have been a real . . .

He struggles until he has regained his composure. Robert stays silent.

Instead, we are stuck with Alderman Duxbury.

ROBERT

I've had my call-up.

GUTHRIE

What?

Robert produces a piece of paper from his pocket.

We must get you deferred.

ROBERT

On what grounds?

GUTHRIE

The choir.

ROBERT

That's not grounds. Music. I'm going to register as a conscientious objector.

This takes Guthrie by surprise –

GUTHRIE

You'll go to prison.

ROBERT

I thought you'd approve.

GUTHRIE

I'm thinking of the choir.

A tiny beat as Robert absorbs this.

ROBERT

Of course you are.

GUTHRIE

Duxbury's on the Appeals Tribunal. He'll get you off.

ROBERT

I don't want him to.

Silence. Then suddenly Guthrie speaks with real force –

GUTHRIE

Fucking war. The vicars want it. The women want it. The idiots getting killed, they want it. Who do you turn to?

Another silence. Guthrie stands to go . . .

ROBERT

I'm sorry about your friend . . . I wish . . . I'd like to help if I can.

GUTHRIE

You could stay out of prison. That would help.

ROBERT

I don't mean that . . . I mean . . . I know you can't just replace one friend with another . . . But . . .

He looks at Guthrie. It's clear what he means. Guthrie looks at the ground. Silence. Finally –

GUTHRIE

I should . . .

He sets off.

ROBERT

Can I ask you something? Why are we doing this? This oratorio about an old man?

Guthrie stops and turns.

GUTHRIE

What do you mean?

ROBERT

It's the young men who are dying.

INT. DUXBURY'S HOUSE, HALL– NIGHT

Duxbury comes into the hall, closing the front door behind him. The house is dark and still.

INT. DUXBURY'S HOUSE, PARLOUR – NIGHT

In the parlour. Duxbury sits at the piano. Mrs Duxbury is in an armchair, staring straight ahead.

Duxbury has the score of Gerontius *on the stand, and is picking out the notes one by one as he tries to make sense of his part. He bangs his hands down on the keys – rather as Guthrie did in the rehearsal room.*

Mrs Duxbury looks at him. Silence. Just the retreating chord.

DUXBURY

This house can't become a mausoleum, Margaret. We can't live in total silence forever.

Mrs Duxbury resumes her staring.

MRS DUXBURY

You're free to live entirely as you please, Bernard.

Silence. Duxbury returns to the piano. He starts to pick out the notes again.

EXT. STATION – DAY

A battalion departs from the station – lots of steam. Younger members of the chorus watch their friends board the train.

ELLIS

The next lot won't be so cheerful.

LOFTY

Why?

ELLIS

Because we won't be volunteers.

Salvation Army band playing, including Mary with Mitch hanging about.

A curate dispensing good cheer: 'Home by Christmas'.

EXT. STATION – DAY

Later. The crowd has gone. A flotilla of nurses waits as another train slides in – a hospital train. The wounded disembark, some stretchered.

One of the walking wounded has lost an arm. Clyde.

EXT. STREET – DAY

Clyde humping his kit bag through the empty streets of Ramsden.

EXT. BELLA'S HOUSE – DAY

Clyde walks up to the front door. Knocks. Bella opens it, wiping her hands.

CLYDE

Hello, stranger.

BELLA

Bloody hell.

She collapses in a dead faint. He rushes towards her.

INT. BELLA'S KITCHEN – DAY

Clyde and Bella. She's recovering with a cup of tea.

CLYDE

I've seen fellas dropping all around me – I've never seen anyone go down like that.

BELLA

I thought you were dead.

A little slightly sticky pause.

What did you do? Were you wounded?

CLYDE

Well, I didn't fall off my bike.

Again, an uncomfortable silence.

Same dirty girl. I hope.

He puts his hand on her thigh, she brushes it off.

BELLA

Don't do that.

CLYDE

Why not? You used to like it.

She stands. He's conscious that this reunion is slipping away from him . . .

Anyway. I'm safe enough now . . . till death fetches me in the proper way.

She moves to the sink with her cup.

I can even come back to the Choral.

She turns quickly.

BELLA

What?

CLYDE

Why not? Give me something to do.

BELLA

You've only one arm.

CLYDE

So what? I'm not conducting the bloody thing.

She turns back, starts to wash the cup.

Be nice. Singing again. Get back to the way things were.

She's not rising to that.

Besides, I know the *Matthew Passion* like the back of my hand.

BELLA

We're not doing the *Matthew Passion.*

CLYDE

Oh?

BELLA

It's something else. You'd have to speak to Guthrie.

CLYDE

Who's he?

BELLA

New Chorus Master. Folk are terrified of him.

CLYDE

I'm just back from the Front, Bella. I think I'll manage.

She drops the cup into the sink. She can't seem to puncture him – and doesn't want to hurt him. There's a painful silence. Finally he stands.

Well . . . I just called in to see if things had changed . . .

She can't turn to face him.

Have they?

Silence. She stares down at the water. He waits until he can bear it no longer.

Cheerio, then.

He goes. Bella starts to weep, softly.

BELLA

(*quietly*)

Cheerio, love.

EXT. TOWN HALL – DAY

Robert and Guthrie going into the main entrance of the Town Hall.

DUXBURY

(V.O.)

Under the Military Service Act, 1916, the Tribunal is now in session.

INT. TOWN HALL COMMITTEE ROOM – DAY

Duxbury, Lady Horsfall, Canon Truelove, Major Dobson are the Tribunal members. Guthrie to one side.

DUXBURY

This isn't particularly formal and of course I know Mr Horner from the Choral Society where he is our much valued pianist. Dr Guthrie has come along just as an observer. I'd rather think of it as a friendly conversation.

MAJOR DOBSON

I wouldn't. This young man is objecting to doing military service.

Canon Truelove reaches for a piece of paper.

CANON TRUELOVE

I have your statement. What puzzles me about you people is that you always think you're privy to the mind of God.

He reads from Robert's statement. The others pick up their copies.

'War is not part of God's plan.' Well, I'm a canon of Ripon Cathedral so I'm more familiar with the mind of God than you are and war does come into God's plan and always has. You've only to read the Old Testament. It's war, war, war.

Guthrie is restive throughout and has to be curbed by Duxbury.

MAJOR DOBSON

I find no sport. Do you do any sport?

ROBERT

Not especially.

MAJOR DOBSON

Not especially.

ROBERT

I prefer music.

MAJOR DOBSON

I wasn't aware they were alternatives.

DUXBURY

Mr Horner is a talented pianist.

LADY HORSFALL

That doesn't stop him kicking a ball.

GUTHRIE

We're talking about firing a gun.

MAJOR DOBSON

You're not talking about anything. You're just an observer.

LADY HORSFALL

I long to serve. I'm a crack shot but the only creatures who get the benefit are the pheasants.

MAJOR DOBSON

Got a girlfriend?

ROBERT

Not as such.

CANON TRUELOVE

Not a vegetarian by any chance?

Robert shakes his head.

Reading your statement, young man, I can't understand how you have any moral compass at all, let alone any contact with sacred music.

ROBERT

I don't rule out serving in another capacity.

MAJOR DOBSON

Oh, that's magnanimous of you. I'm sure Field Marshal Haig will be relieved to know that.

ROBERT

I thought I could be a stretcher bearer.

LADY HORSFALL

You don't seem to be aware that you belong to a privileged generation, the first in our island's history to be granted the honour of being conscripted. I would be proud.

DUXBURY

Knowing Mr Horner, I think I would advise the Tribunal that you would benefit from a brief period of deferment – say three months for you to think it over.

ROBERT

I've made up my mind.

Duxbury looks despairingly at Guthrie.

DUXBURY

Then I will put it to the Chorus Master. Is Mr Horner essential to the society's next concert?

GUTHRIE

He is.

ROBERT

No.

DUXBURY

You should be grateful you're needed. There's lads going off every day. Nobody needs them.

LADY HORSFALL

Except the country. I'd be happy to go.

INT. TOWN HALL STAIRCASE AND LOBBY – DAY

Robert and Guthrie are coming down the grand staircase.

GUTHRIE

Duxbury wanted to help. You have to learn to play the game. Don't spit on your luck.

ROBERT

I don't want any special treatment. I'm happy to be a conchy.

GUTHRIE

Well, what about the choir?

ROBERT

That's all you care about. You, you're no different from the bloody generals. You're single minded. Single minded. That's what's wrong with the world.

GUTHRIE

You're young. That's what's wrong.

ROBERT

You sound like Duxbury. Or Field Marshal Haig.

Guthrie pushes open the door to the Concert Hall.

INT. CONCERT HALL – DAY

Guthrie and Robert in the empty Concert Hall.

GUTHRIE

In less than a month's time we hope this hall will be full and Alderman Duxbury has yet to give us even an approximation of the notes.

INT. REHEARSAL ROOM – DAY

Clyde sings with Robert's accompaniment. Guthrie sits listening.

Clyde has a beautiful tenor voice. He sings with real feeling 'Where'er You Walk' (from Handel's Semele).

He finishes. Silence. Guthrie is impressed. And moved.

At the back of the hall we see Duxbury. He too was transported – but his face is darkened with worry. He leaves without being noticed.

INT. REHEARSAL ROOM – DAY

Robert has gone. Just Guthrie and Clyde sitting at the table.

GUTHRIE

What do you mean, you don't want it?

CLYDE

I don't.

GUTHRIE

Then why audition?

Clyde stares at the table.

CLYDE

I used to love the Choral. When it was Bella and me. I can't see her every day, though. Not without . . . It'll drive me distracted.

Silence.

GUTHRIE

You've been dealt some rough cards.

Clyde nods furiously. Still focused on the tabletop.

I'm going to say something now. It may seem insensitive, but . . . art is insensitive. Ironically. You've all the ingredients here for genius.

Clyde looks at him.

Heartbroken. Limb lost. Not to mention the things you've seen . . .

CLYDE

I'd rather be . . . happy.

GUTHRIE

Well. So would every other bugger. Elgar included.

Silence. Guthrie is soft, paternal.

But there are people who – funnily enough – would give their right arm to be able to do what you can do.

Clyde looks at him.

And I don't know whether it's cruel or kind, but life has offered you a consolation prize. And now – at your lowest – is the moment you're best equipped to use it.

CLYDE

Life's fucking shit.

Guthrie nods. Total, profound agreement.

GUTHRIE

So sing.

EXT. MRS BISHOP'S HOUSE – DAY

Mrs Bishop opens the door to Duxbury.

MRS BISHOP

It isn't Tuesday?

DUXBURY

I know. I'm sorry.

MRS BISHOP

Come in then. Hanging about on the doorstep, what does it look like?

INT. MRS BISHOP'S HOUSE HALLWAY – DAY

Fytton appears down the stairs in his shirt tails.

FYTTON

How many more times, you're not having Fridays.

DUXBURY

Just this once. Guthrie wants to see me.

FYTTON

No. We agreed.

MRS BISHOP

Neither of you will be having anything unless you behave yourselves.

EXT. MRS BISHOP'S HOUSE – DAY

Fytton now dressed, with Mrs Bishop at the door.

MRS BISHOP

Come back at teatime.

Fytton goes, looking murderous.

INT. QUEENS' HOTEL – DAY

Guthrie and Duxbury, the tearoom empty.

DUXBURY

He's too young. His voice isn't heavy enough. It's an old man dying – I can play older. He can't.

GUTHRIE

The lad has the voice of an angel. Bernard . . .

DUXBURY

Alderman. I don't want you appealing to my better nature. Like you, I don't have one.

Duxbury thinks for a moment.

It's this flaming war. It's ruined everything. We used to have such a nice going-on. It's my own fault, appointing you in the first place. If I cared less about the music I could put my foot down. Others would.

GUTHRIE

I know . . .

Guthrie puts his hand on Duxbury's shoulder.

We're still short of a devil.

DUXBURY

Is there a solo devil?

GUTHRIE

The way we're doing it, yes, and it's got you written all over it.

Guthrie pats him on the shoulder.

DUXBURY

I wish I didn't like singing.

INT. REHEARSAL ROOM – DAY

Rehearsal with full chorus. The string trio from Collinson's also present.

GUTHRIE

Ladies and gentlemen, we have a new Gerontius.

Clyde stands, and the chorus applauds. Duxbury, now seated with the tenors in the chorus, lowers his head. Clyde glances at Bella. She snaps her head away, fast. He carries on looking.

But in the absence of a full symphony orchestra and a chorus of a hundred, we must tailor Elgar's *Dream* to our present circumstances. To begin with, our Gerontius isn't old. He's a young man. Who's dying nowadays? Not the old. He's a soldier. And perhaps the angel who delivers him from purgatory is a nurse. And Heaven, if not quite the presence of God, is home and England, and peace.

MRS PEMBERTON

What about the orchestra?

MISS NINER

We may be a chamber ensemble but I don't think there will be any complaints.

GUTHRIE

It will be quite short and not a full-blown oratorio by any manner of means, but it will be as heartfelt as that original one in Birmingham Town Hall. Less holy maybe, but more topical.

TRICKETT

(*sotto voce to Duxbury*)

But is it Elgar?

Guthrie lifts his baton.

Clyde sings, accompanied by Robert at the piano and the string trio. Segue into practice and rehearsal sequence:

EXT. DUXBURY'S MILL – DAY

During their midday dinner break, Mary, Bella, Flo and three or four of the younger choir members huddle outside the mill learning their parts.

INT. DUXBURY'S MILL WASHROOM – DAY

At the end of the day, Ellis, Mitch and some of the younger men sing from Gerontius *while they wash.*

EXT. DUXBURY'S MILL – DAY

As the mill workers leave they pass Duxbury, wishing him good evening. He is buried in the score, oblivious.

EXT. TERRACE OF HOUSES – DAY

Lofty delivering telegrams, cycling down a street with lines of washing hung across, singing, score on his handlebars.

INT. BAKERY – DAY

Podge checking a row of newly iced cakes, then singing from a Gerontius *score, the other baker looking on askance.*

EXT. MILL DAM – DAY

The young chorus members swimming in the mill dam, and sunbathing with the score, singing. Clyde on the bank, watching.

INT. REHEARSAL ROOM – DAY

Another rehearsal. We have the exhilarating impression that it's starting to come together. Guthrie is conducting with gusto – and looks as though he's even enjoying himself . . .

GUTHRIE

Good! Good!

The music stops. Guthrie is pleased.

I'm proud of you. Elgar would be proud of you. Two weeks to go, and we're finally getting somewhere . . .

A big moment. The clergyman from the committee speaks up.

REVEREND CRABTREE

I'm still not happy about purgatory.

A groan from the choir.

I appreciate that the author is Roman Catholic, but the Church of England is very clear. There's no such place as purgatory.

CLYDE

(from the front of the room)

No such place? Listen, I could take you there tomorrow. Because purgatory starts ten yards from the front line. And it's called No Man's Land. Every time we mount another damn fool attack we cross it if we're lucky. That's purgatory. There's some flounder through it and there's some drown in it. Some try and crawl out and get driven back by their officers, them as well as us – and get shot if they don't. That's purgatory.

Silence. No one knows quite what to say.

INT. PUB – NIGHT

Later that night. Members of the choir singing a popular song.

Clyde standing alone at the bar. Lofty, Ellis and Mitch come over. Lofty pulls out an envelope with his call-up papers.

CLYDE

When did these arrive?

ELLIS

This morning.

LOFTY

(*producing his papers*)

Me an' all.

MITCH

And me. We're to report to the station the week after the medical.

ELLIS

Were you a good soldier?

CLYDE

Yes. I didn't get killed.

MITCH

Just lost an arm.

CLYDE

When you're over there, see if you can find it.

LOFTY

If there's time, I'd like to see a bit of the countryside.

CLYDE

If there's a half day, you mean?

Mary passes them –

MARY

War, war, war. You lot talk about nothing else.

MITCH

Shall I see you home?

MARY

No fear.

Mary walks on. Mitch shoves his hands in his pockets.

MITCH

I'm not getting anywhere, am I?

ELLIS

I don't know what you see in her. She won't even let you kiss her.

MITCH

That's what I see in her.

A woman's voice from behind.

WOMAN'S VOICE

(*O.S.*)

Oi!

The lads look round.

ELLIS

Shit.

MITCH

What?

ELLIS

It's her mother.

They run off, laughing – leaving Mitch standing as the woman approaches.

MARY'S MOTHER

Is it you that's courting our Mary?

MITCH

I . . . I don't know what you're talking about.

MARY'S MOTHER

You know full well. Answer me. Yes or no.

MITCH

We haven't done anything. I mean . . . kissed even.

MARY'S MOTHER

That doesn't surprise me. She takes after her grandma. Nobody ever laid a finger on her either.

MITCH

Except her grandpa presumably.

MARY'S MOTHER

You cheeky sod. Still, I wish you well.

MITCH

What at?

MARY'S MOTHER

Routing the Salvation Army. I'd outlaw that tambourine. I don't mind Jesus, but not while we're having our tea.

MITCH

Sounds as if I'd have been better off with you.

MARY'S MOTHER

Steady on.

She walks past him. Stops.

It'll be all right. Jesus is just a phase. I've never fancied him as a son-in-law.

She goes. Mitch beams.

EXT. MOORS – DAY

Clyde and Bella.

Silence.

CLYDE

I don't mind about Ellis.

She looks at him. Surprised.

He's right enough. If you're happy.

BELLA

I am.

Silence.

Are you all right, love?

CLYDE

I didn't think it would make that much difference. But it's surprising how much you need both of them.

They share – not a laugh, exactly – but a smile maybe.

There is one thing.

BELLA

What?

CLYDE

I don't want to ask.

BELLA

Nay, go on. If I can help I will.

He looks down at his crotch.

CLYDE

I can't do it with the left hand. It gets tired.

She gets it. She's not appalled – but she looks around.

BELLA

No, Clyde . . .

CLYDE

Please. You never minded before.

BELLA

I have to think of Ellis.

CLYDE

Just the one. I'll train myself to do it with the other. I can if I set my mind to it. Please.

A moment. Then, she reaches to his flies and unbuttons them . . .

EXT. MOORS – DAY

Bella is walking away. We're with Clyde. He drops his head into his hand and weeps.

INT. REHEARSAL ROOM – DAY

Guthrie and Robert working at the piano, going through the score, cutting and rearranging. Mary listening.

ROBERT

He must be a decent chap.

GUTHRIE

Who?

ROBERT

Elgar.

GUTHRIE

Decent? I don't know. Magnificent, yes. Inspirational . . .

ROBERT

Generous enough to let us tinker with his stuff.

GUTHRIE

'Tinker'? 'Tinker'? Re-imagine. 'Tinker'.

Pause.

ROBERT

You haven't told him, have you?

GUTHRIE

He gave his permission.

ROBERT

I mean all this new carry-on. No orchestra. The cutting. The rearrangement.

GUTHRIE

I haven't got round to it. We're a fiddling little minor provincial choral society. He won't want bothering.

MARY

It's only an hour away.

GUTHRIE

What is?

MARY

Manchester. They're giving him an honorary degree.

GUTHRIE

I saw.

MARY

The day of the concert. We could ask him to come.

GUTHRIE

Certainly not. This is a great man. He's got better things to do.

ROBERT

He's an old man. Maybe he hasn't.

GUTHRIE

Be told, the pair of you. Save your bright ideas for adapting the score.

ROBERT

Well, I've got another suggestion. Why can't the characters dress up – Clyde as a soldier. Mary as a nurse.

GUTHRIE

This is an oratorio. Dressing up is opera.

ROBERT

We've broken some rules, so why can't we break others?

Guthrie looks at him.

GUTHRIE

You're right. After all, we're nobody. Gerontius is a cripple in his late teens, the orchestra is the trio from the Queens' Hotel . . . Opera, oratorio – who's going to care?

MARY

You're not nobody.

GUTHRIE

I am now. I was somebody once, although that was in Germany. Not now.

He pats Robert on the shoulder and leaves.

MARY

He must like you. I've never known him accept a suggestion from anyone else. Ever.

ROBERT

He does like me, I suppose.

MARY

(*quietly*)

I do too.

ROBERT

What?

She shakes her head. Nothing.

MARY

I already wrote that letter.

ROBERT

To Elgar? No.

MARY

Why not?

ROBERT

We're not ready. Nowhere near.

MARY

He'll understand.

ROBERT

Elgar? Why should he? He's – he's Elgar.

MARY

Well, I've done it now. Sorry. Sorry, Robert.

INT. MUNICIPAL BUILDING – DAY

A medical in progress. Line of men, naked to the waist.

ELLIS

They'll fail Podge.

LOFTY

Why?

ELLIS

He was in our class at school. He had fits. You had to get something between his teeth.

The doctor comes over, reading Podge's medical records.

DOCTOR

Is this right? Are you epileptic?

PODGE

Only occasionally. Not so as to stop me shooting Fritz.

The doctor gives him his papers back.

LOFTY

Why does he look at your willy?

ELLIS

The clap.

LOFTY

Me? Fat chance.

EXT. TOWN HALL – DAY

A banner across the front of the Town Hall: RAMSDEN CHORAL SOCIETY – THE DREAM OF GERONTIUS BY SIR EDWARD ELGAR.

Lofty and Ellis arriving with their bikes. The rest of the chorus arriving slowly. One of the sopranos has brought her small daughter. Podge has a box of cakes.

ELLIS

You jammy sod.

PODGE

Why? I want to go. I shouldn't have said. Fits. They're nothing. Once they're done fighting they'll be wanting a scone.

Trickett dives into the cake box.

TRICKETT

Are these for us?

PODGE

That's a Battenberg.

TRICKETT

(*mouth full*)

I'm surprised you're still making these. German muck.

PODGE

I wanted to go to war but I still don't understand why we're killing folks who like the same fancies as we do. I mean, we've got common ground.

A Rolls-Royce slides into view. The chauffeur emerges with a rug and opens the door. An oldish man gets out, adorned in the ceremonial gown of a doctor of music.

ELGAR

Is Dr Guthrie about?

ELLIS

Certainly. Of course. This way.

Leaving the others admiring the car.

MITCH

Nice frock.

Which the chauffeur overhears.

LOFTY

How much do they cost, this model?

CHAUFFEUR

Why? Are you thinking of getting one?

INT. TOWN HALL LOBBY – DAY

Elgar sweeps down the corridor towards the Concert Hall followed by Ellis and the others, now catching up with them. From within, the sound of the piano and string trio rehearsing.

INT. TOWN HALL CONCERT HALL – DAY

Elgar enters, more members of the Choral gathering around him. Mary comes quickly over. Guthre and Robert on the platform at the far end of the hall, working at the piano with the trio, oblivious.

MARY

May I assist you, sir?

ELGAR

You're in the Salvation Army.

MARY

I am, though it's not popular.

ELGAR

I thought that was the point of it.

MARY

With the choir. They don't like me singing on street corners. I don't mind where I sing.

ELGAR

Make a joyful noise unto the Lord.

MARY

Exactly.

BELLA

You don't want a cup of tea?

ELGAR

No. I want Dr Guthrie, and I don't have a lot of time.

Guthrie hurries over with Robert clutching the score.

GUTHRIE

Sir Edward . . .

ELGAR

Dr Guthrie? Elgar.

GUTHRIE

I'm astonished.

ELGAR

At my get-up? I've been in Manchester.

They shake hands.

China, is it, where every profession has its own uniform? Well, this is mine. My musical degree. In the circumstances I feel it's quite discreet. I certainly don't feel drab.

GUTHRIE

No.

ELGAR

Composing is a noble profession. It is romantic, adventurous and poorly paid. But for once this afternoon I am allowed to advertise. I'm not just a jumped-up shop assistant.

GUTHRIE

Who thinks that?

ELGAR

I do, for one. At thirty-four I was still serving behind the counter in my father's shop.

GUTHRIE

But you're knighted.

ELGAR

Knighted, yes, but what has happened to the peerage? Still I am a humble man and this is what one appreciates. To have my work performed by amateurs – talented amateurs, I'm sure – in the back of beyond, that is the real distinction. And don't worry, I shall not be attending the performance. And I don't expect too much. Nothing can be worse than the *Dream*'s first outing when I ran from Birmingham Town Hall with my hands over my ears. Supposedly a glimpse of heaven, it was diabolical.

Ellis turns to Lofty.

ELLIS

(*under his breath*)

Never mind composing, he certainly fucking talks.

LOFTY

(*under his breath*)

If he wants a preview, we're in the shit.

Back to Elgar . . .

ELGAR

I was touched you should want to put it on. Few societies do, amateurs not at all. I don't have a lot of time but is there any chance of you giving me a hint of what you've been doing?

LOFTY

Shit.

GUTHRIE

I wish I could but – tonight is our performance, and we have much to do.

ELGAR

No matter. Just an old man's vanity. I'm not as popular as I was. *Pomp and Circumstance* notwithstanding.

GUTHRIE

Besides, the choir has been rehearsing all morning – I've sent most of them home.

ELGAR

Not even the young lady?

GUTHRIE

She's not prepared.

MARY

I could do something. I'd like to.

ELGAR

There you are. If she sings as delightfully as she looks it will be a treat.

Mary and Robert run up onto the stage.

She sings 'The Angel's Farewell'. Elgar is impressed.

'Softly and gently, dearly ransomed soul,
In my most loving arms I now enfold thee . . .'

He goes over to the stage and kisses her hand.

Now I must go.

The chauffeur brings in Elgar's travelling coat and helps him out of his doctoral robes, which he is putting over his arm. Except that even now Elgar doesn't wish to be parted from them and puts them over his own arm.

Trickett is next to Mrs Bishop.

TRICKETT

(*quietly*)

Forget the dressing-gown and he just looks like anybody else.

MRS BISHOP

My late father-in-law springs to mind.

As Elgar and the chauffeur reach the doors of the Concert Hall, Duxbury pushes forward.

DUXBURY

(*to Elgar*)

I'm sure you must be weary of your fans, Sir Edward, but could I trouble you to sign my score?

ELGAR

Of course. And the young lady's.

MARY

Please.

ELGAR

Are you in the chorus?

DUXBURY

No. I'm actually one of the principals. In fact I was singing Gerontius until we brought it up to date.

ELGAR

Up to date?

ELLIS

Oh fuck.

DUXBURY

Less . . . religious.

ELGAR

But it's Newman's poem. That's why it's religious. So who is Gerontius?

CLYDE

I am.

Elgar stares.

ELGAR

But he's . . .

Elgar looks down and shakes Clyde's remaining hand.

(*to Guthrie*)

No. No. He's too young.

GUTHRIE

He was wounded at Ypres.

ELGAR

I don't care if he was wounded at Agincourt. His voice won't be heavy enough.

GUTHRIE

You would be surprised, Sir Edward, how poignant a young man sounds – especially in our present moment.

ELGAR

What else have you meddled with? Let me see the score.

Robert brings him the conductor's score. He flicks through it.

This is disgraceful. I hardly recognise it. This isn't a score, it's a doily. Will the tenor be in uniform?

CLYDE

This is my costume.

ELGAR

Costume? This is an oratorio. It isn't fancy dress. And what about the orchestra?

MISS NINER

We are doing the music, Sir Edward, our trio.

ELGAR

A trio?

MISS NINER

Would you like us to play you an extract? We've never had any complaints.

Elgar takes Guthrie and Robert aside.

ELGAR

I can't have this. I thought I was doing you a favour.

GUTHRIE

You are. It's an interpretation. Art comes out of art.

ELGAR

Not out of mine.

GUTHRIE

It's your music, even if it's not your story.

ELGAR

Cardinal Newman's story.

GUTHRIE

The young man is dying. Why would he be dying these days except in the trenches, like all the rest? Hundreds of them? One after the other. Dying in ditches – and on the seas.

ELGAR

One death tells you more than a thousand. So much for bringing it up to date. And I wouldn't place too much reliance on the war. I sat next to Field Marshal Haig at the Academy Dinner and he told me in confidence that it will all be over within six months. You won't look so up to date then.

Elgar sweeps out. Guthrie hurries Mary towards the main door.

GUTHRIE

Speak to him. He likes your voice. You're a good-looking girl. Be nice to him.

EXT. TOWN HALL – DAY

Mary rushes towards Elgar, who is about to get into the car. The rest follow.

ELGAR

I'm sorry, my dear, but I cannot allow them to do it. I have my reputation to think of. Whereas you, you're wasted here. It's a good voice. It should be better trained. I know teachers who can help. Your voice. It's God-given.

He takes her hand.

MARY

I'm not a proper singer.

ELGAR

You could be.

MARY

I'm just in the mill. I can't afford to—

ELGAR

Don't worry about that.

MARY

If I said yes, would you . . .

He says nothing.

Some of these boys won't be coming back.

She disengages his hand.

Duxbury pushes forward a small child (the soprano's daughter who arrived at the start of the scene); she embarks on 'Land of Hope and Glory', which Elgar plainly doesn't want to hear.

Elgar gets into his car.

DUXBURY

She hasn't finished.

ELGAR

I know the rest.

Guthrie hammers on the window. Elgar lowers it.

GUTHRIE

Your first big success – triumph really – was your *Variations on an Original Theme*. The *Enigma Variations*.

ELGAR

So?

GUTHRIE

And you didn't write the theme yourself.

ELGAR

Possibly. It's not important.

GUTHRIE

You were building on someone else's work, we were building on yours.

Elgar instructs the chauffeur and the car starts off. Guthrie shouts after the retreating car.

Art does come out of art . . . even yours.

But he's gone. The child is still labouring through 'Land of Hope and Glory'.

MOTHER

That's enough, love.

CHILD

Did he not like it?

MOTHER

He loved it.

MITCH

That's it then, is it?

ELLIS

The miserable sod. Nothing to look forward to now.

LOFTY

(*cheerfully, without irony*)

Oh, I don't know. There's France.

DUXBURY

Well, we had a good try.

GUTHRIE

My fault. Don't repeat yourself – the lesson. Once, even at Nuremberg – enough.

He turns slowly away, heading back for the hall.

MARY

Well, I must say, I'm very disappointed.

GUTHRIE

We're all disappointed, my dear.

MARY

No. In you.

Bella comes to join her.

BELLA

I agree.

MARY

It seems such a shame, after all the work we've done.

BELLA

And the boys are going tomorrow.

LOFTY

It's meant a lot to us, Mr Guthrie.

MITCH

It's been a distraction.

ELLIS

It's more than that. Does anyone here feel that we're done with *The Dream of Gerontius*? We can walk away and leave it at that?

No one does.

MARY

He said we can't perform it in public, but . . . Doesn't mean we can't perform it, does it?

CLYDE

Don't let us down, Mr Guthrie.

BELLA

Please.

CLYDE

It matters.

Guthrie manages only an almost imperceptible nod.

INT. TOWN HALL CONCERT HALL – EVENING

Music . . . The Dream of Gerontius *starts.*

The choir and string trio in position, Robert at the piano and Guthrie poised at the music stand.

They start to sing.

EXT. TOWN HALL – EVENING

Outside, we can see the lit hall and hear the music.

INT. TOWN HALL CONCERT HALL – EVENING

The choir singing. Clyde begins his aria. We see Duxbury listening.

EXT. TOWN HALL – EVENING

People are gathering to listen. There are one or two wounded soldiers, and a number of older women and women in mourning. They are drawn through the main doors.

INT. TOWN HALL CONCERT HALL – EVENING

The oratorio coming to an end. Guthrie conducts the final strains. There are tears in his eyes. They finish. Silence.

Guthrie looks up at the choir but is incapable of saying anything. No one knows what to do. After a second, he sweeps his score off the stand and heads for the door.

INT. TOWN HALL LOBBY – EVENING

As Guthrie rushes from the building, he's astonished to see the assembly. Even more astonished to hear them burst into applause . . .

INT. TOWN HALL CONCERT HALL – EVENING

The choir, still in their positions after Guthrie's sudden departure, hear the applause. They look at each other in amazement. Some break into smiles.

LOFTY

Bloody hell.

They rush to the door . . .

INT. TOWN HALL LOBBY – EVENING

The Choral come out – mingling with the assembled crowd – more applause.

Duxbury sees Mrs Duxbury has been standing there, listening. Her eyes are red. He takes her in his arms and the two of them weep.

We see smiling faces – Lofty, Mitch, Fytton, Mary, Bella, Flo, Trickett, Duxbury . . .

INT. FYTTON'S PHOTOGRAPHIC STUDIO AND SHOP – DAY

We see a montage of the new recruits posing for photographs in their uniforms: Ellis, then Mitch, then finally Lofty. The flashbulbs go – bang, bang, bang.

INT. MARY'S HOUSE PARLOUR – NIGHT

Mitch in uniform but in his shirt sleeves, his arm around Mary on the settee. Light kissing. Mary struggles free.

MARY

My mam'll be coming back.

MITCH

Nay, she won't. She's gone to the pictures specially. That's why she lit the fire.

MARY

She's on your side. She's never liked me being in the Army either.

MITCH

What do you think? Come on, love. We're off tomorrow.

MARY

They all say it's not very nice first time.

MITCH

It'll be all right.

MARY

Only I've asked God and if I don't do it, you'll be safe. If I do this for God, he'll do this for me.

MITCH

Nay, Mary. If God is like that you'll be better off without him.

They sit in silence. Mitch leaps up, startling Mary slightly.

MARY

What are you doing?

Mitch doesn't answer. He starts to remove his clothes. Mary is astonished. She looks away. Soon he's naked. He moves to face her, the fire behind him.

MITCH

Look.

MARY

No.

MITCH

This is me, Mary. This is what I look like. I want you to see. Before I go. I want you to see me.

After a while she looks up. They stay like that staring at each other for a while. Then – she looks down again.

Mitch waits, then picks up his clothes and walks out of the room.

Mary stares into the fire, tears forming. She hears the door slam.

EXT. SULLIVAN STREET – NIGHT

Lofty in uniform going down Sullivan Street. Knocks on door.

LOFTY

Hello.

Mrs Bishop opens the door.

MRS BISHOP

Stanley? Is it you? Oh God.

LOFTY

It's all right, Mrs Bishop. I haven't got a telegram.

MRS BISHOP

What is it you want? Your Mam'd play pop.

LOFTY

Can I not come in? It's important.

MRS BISHOP

What for?

She lets him in.

INT. MRS BISHOP'S HOUSE HALLWAY – NIGHT

Lofty doesn't say anything.

MRS BISHOP

You're a bit young.

LOFTY

I'm old enough.

MRS BISHOP

I know your Irene. I used to push your pram.

LOFTY

We're going tomorrow. I've got the money. Do I have to take my shoes off?

MRS BISHOP

Not unless you want to.

She fetches a coat-hanger.

Here's a coat-hanger. You don't want to spoil your new uniform. It looks nice.

LOFTY

Shall I take it off?

MRS BISHOP

Yes, love. Go upstairs.

LOFTY

Mrs Bishop. I don't just want . . . to do it. I'd like to see you and everything.

MRS BISHOP

You shall.

INT. MRS BISHOP'S HOUSE, BEDROOM – NIGHT

Later. Lofty is dressing. He tries to give her some money.

MRS BISHOP

No, love. It's on the house.

LOFTY

Are you sure?

MRS BISHOP

You can come again. When you come back.

LOFTY

Don't let on to our Irene.

(*shaking hands*)

Thank you very much.

MRS BISHOP

Be careful, love. Over there.

LOFTY

I will.

EXT. STATION – DAY

Train in. All the choir getting into one compartment.

ELLIS

(*saying goodbye to Bella*)

Well, I expect he's right – I mean, he'd know, wouldn't he?

BELLA

Who?

ELLIS

Elgar. The whole thing'll probably be over by the time we get there. That's what Field Marshal Haig told him.

BELLA

Just . . . think on. And be careful.

LOFTY

Don't be surprised if I come back with a French girl.

Mrs Bishop alone but waving to various carriages. Mary waves shyly to Mitch. He waves back.

A new telegram boy, still too young to be a conscript, is there with Lofty's bike.

INT. REFRESHMENT ROOM – DAY

Robert is sitting with Guthrie.

ROBERT

I don't suppose there'll be much music. Still, it might do me good to . . . pursue other . . .

He falls into silence.

Two military policemen come in.

GUTHRIE

Here are your friends. Good luck.

ROBERT

Can I just . . .

They stop. Robert faces Guthrie. They look at each other. Robert extends his hand. Guthrie shakes it.

Guthrie framed in the window watching Robert being led away.

EXT. STATION – DAY

On the platform, Duxbury is watching them go. He stands in silence, alone as the couples kiss and the boys wave. Finally Guthrie comes up to him.

DUXBURY

I came down when our Arnold went. There was a band then. The Lord Mayor. Now there's not even a curate.

The train pulls out of the station.

Fade to black.